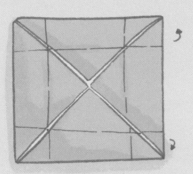

10. Unfold the top and bottom.

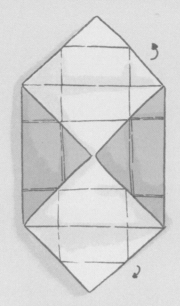

11. Open the top and bottom triangles so the paper looks like this.

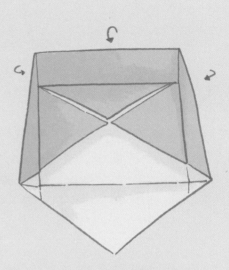

12. Move the top inwards and lift the sides, tucking the folds at the corners inside, to make the walls of the box.

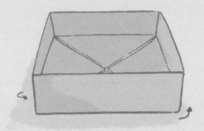

13. Do the same to the bottom part.

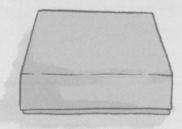

14. Now repeat, using a slightly smaller square of paper so that you have a bottom of your box and a lid.

15. Draw your nightmare (make sure it's extra yummy).

16. Put it in your box.

17. Leave your closed box outside your door.

18. If you don't want to make a box, just fold your drawing and address it to the Night Bear.

To Tom and Billie, the tastiest little nightmares

First published in Great Britain in 2019
by Andersen Press Ltd.,
20 Vauxhall Bridge Road, London SW1V 2SA.

First edition.
Printed and bound in China.
British Library Cataloguing in Publication Data available.
ISBN 978 1 78344 714 5

The Night Bear

Ana & Thiago de Moraes

Andersen Press

At night, when it's dark and quiet,
the Night Bear hops onto a night
bus and sets off to find his dinner.

NB

SWEET SHOP –
PLAYGROUND – MARKET –
SHOP – FOOTBALL PITCH –
GREEN – ZOO – LIDO –
BANDSTAND – FOREST –
NIGHT BEAR MOUNTAINS

THE CITY

Tonight he is in luck:
lots of children have
left nightmares out.
And nightmares are
the Night Bear's
favourite food.

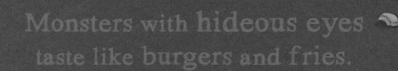

Monsters with hideous eyes
taste like burgers and fries.

Storms that **bang** and **crash**
taste like **sausage** and **mash**.

Dragons with a fiery bite taste like
Turkish Delight.

Scary pirates being **mean** taste like
strawberries and cream.

Unicorns and rainbows taste like... **wait...**

The night bus will be back soon,
thank goodness. But it does seem a
waste to throw away a whole dream...

So the Night Bear goes from street to street,
looking for someone who might like **unicorns** and **rainbows**.

All the children seem to be asleep.
Until he gets to Tom's house.

He's never seen
a dreamer up
close before.

This one doesn't
have much fur and
is quite small.

He clearly doesn't
eat enough yummy
nightmares.

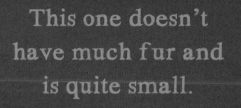

"Would you like this?"
asks the Night Bear.
"Can I have a look?"
asks Tom.

"Rainbows and unicorns!" cries Tom.
"I know," says the Night Bear.
"Really yucky."

"Would you like **this**?" asks Tom.
"It's **really** horrible."
The Night Bear open**s** the box...

"Spiders and a giant snake!" (They taste like chocolate cake.)
The perfect pudding to end the evening.

Happy with their new dreams,
boy and Bear say goodnight.

As the bears wait for the night bus,
the Night Bear tells the others about
his funny new friend, who had fur
only on the top of his head and
a very strange taste in dreams.

And if, like Tom, you are not too keen
on nightmares, then sweet dreams,
sleep tight, hope the Night Bear
comes tonight.

The Night Bear's Favourite Snacks

Cyclopes of doom taste like delicious mushrooms.

Evil witches taste like egg sandwiches.

Bloodthirsty bats taste like bacon baps.

Banshees that scream taste like custard creams.

A scary yeti tastes like yummy spaghetti.

Slimy slugs taste like coffee in mugs.

Scary puppets taste like chicken nuggets.

Angry gnomes taste like ice cream cones.

Pterodactlys in the sky taste like apple pie.

Monsters from the lake taste like juicy steak.

Giant poodles taste like ramen noodles.

The Ogre of Fart tastes like lemon tart.

Bandit queens taste like baked beans.

Sharks with pointy teeth taste like roast beef.

Robbers wearing bandanas taste like ripe bananas.

A howling ghost tastes like cheese on toast.